And Then There Were Two

Wilma Miller

authorHOUSE®

AuthorHouse™
1663 Liberty Drive
Bloomington, IN 47403
www.authorhouse.com
Phone: 1 (800) 839-8640

Published by AuthorHouse 10/16/2015

ISBN: 978-1-5049-5713-7 (sc)
ISBN: 978-1-5049-5712-0 (e)

Prologue

Wilma was one of a large family from the deep South who survived the Great Depression in the early thirties. Then relived the tragedies of World War II. With faith and courage relived. With love that endured and the sacrifices that her family faced and yet came through victorious.

Dedications/Acknowledgements

To my dear mama and daddy who sacrificed for me. Who loved me and led me on the path in life to be happy and succeed in all that I endeavored to do.

Also my dear sisters and brothers for loving me and keeping me safe.

To all the ministers and people of faith who helped me spiritually that gave me a firm foundation as I pass through this life.

I also want to thank my sister Ruby Smith for standing with me and encouraging me to pass on this true story. Our hope is that someone will use this book to encourage others gleen hope to face their future.

And Then There Were Two

Being born in a small rural community, one of sixteen children, there were many trials, hardships and disappointments, but many happy times as well. We all learned to love, share and to work hard and were taught right from wrong.

My daddy was from a resourceful and financially secure family who knew nothing of hardships, was well educated and extremely brilliant.

Just the opposite was my mama who was born to a very poor family. They were known as sharecroppers. However, this family had a pretty young girl named Mary.

One day the father of this poor family approached my daddy and asked if he could live on his land, be furnished a house for his family to live in, work the land, and share the profits that they produced. It was agreed upon and the move began immediately.

As they were moving in my daddy noticed this pretty young girl they called Mary with her family.

While daddy was from a privileged background, handsome, masculine and considered a good catch for any girl.

Being interested in what he saw of Mary he would surely get to know her. He continued to observe her as she grew older, paying special attention to all of her features, her thick dark hair, her fair alabaster skin, deep blue eyes and most of all her fast maturing body. She being much younger than he, but very smitten with her already. As he laid in bed at night he would visualize just how he would approach her to become friends with her.

Needless to say in a shy way she was already looking and admiring his good looks.

Then came the day when she was helping his mother he seized the chance to approach her with conversation. This led to him asking her if she would give him the honor of seeing her from time to time, yet all the time she was so thrilled at being noticed by him. Her answer to him was, yes I think I would like that. As time went on they were often seen together. Finally daddy got up the nerve to ask her if he could take her to church, so with so much pride she agreed, and from then forward they developed a wonderful relationship.

As the weeks and months passed they were inseperable. Then one night he was taking her home from church, he, in his heart, realized he could wait no longer and at her front door he dropped to one knee, holding her hand, and with all of his love pouring out the words came, Mary, my sweet Mary will you marry me? I want to be with you for the rest of my life. As he knelt there waiting for her answer it seemed his heart stood still. Then at that very minute he could hear the voice of an angel saying, yes, yes Marsh. I love you so much, I will be your wife. They then caressed and with a lingering goodnight kiss they departed, each heart filled with love. Even though Mary was only fifteen years old she knew the true meaning of love and being loved. She knew too that her life would not be complete without him.

As she entered the house her maw could see a special look on her face. Before she could even ask anything, Mary shouted in almost an uncontrollable voice, Marsh has asked me to marry him. Yet a happy feeling for Mary she slowly spoke to Mary saying saying, now baby girl this is a big decision for you but I trust you. You know your own heart and I know you will make the right decision. To this Mary explained, maw I love him with all my heart and I will make him a good wife, and I know he loves me dearly. And Mary, her maw continued, your paw will have to be told. While you do have my blessing, you must have his also.

The next morning Mary arose early with nothing on her mind but Marsh, and all the plans she would be making. First she would tell Marsh that she wanted him to ask paw for permission to marry her, which she did that day.

The next day would seem like an eternity for Marsh until he would see Mary again. As the evening was approaching he found himself rapidly making preparations to see his sweet Mary. In his Model T automobile he made his way to Mary's house. Arriving there he was asked by maw to come in. Before he was seated Mary spoke softly to Marsh asking him if he would speak privately to paw. Marsh motioned slightly with his hand as Mary left the room and paw entered. Marsh stood nervously before paw not knowing what his reactions would be, but knowing too this session must take place. Marsh already knew Mary's family and also knew that they were good church going people so with his best manners and trying to control his nerves he began, Mr. Davis sir, I am truly in love with Mary and I have come here tonight to ask your permission to marry her. With this paw raised his eyebrows, cleared his throat and said, I realize that I will be losing my little girl, but being happy for Mary he graciously said yes, I will be honored to have you as my son-in-law. From that day forward the wedding plans began. Together Mary and Marsh would choose a date for the wedding. Mary and maw would choose the fabric for the dress and it would surely be white for Mary was truly a virgin. The veil would be small because Mary was such a petite little girl and of a church wedding, and blessed by the heavens above. Mary's dress would be sewn by maw and from the finest fabric they could afford. With Mary's size and shape she would look like an angel walking on earth. Marsh would not give thought to anything but Mary, however he would be dressed in his finest, because he was so proud of Mary and wanted her to be proud of him.

The wedding day had finally arrived and the young couple was deliriously happy. The little church was beautifully decorated as this was the most prominent wedding of the season. All of the family and friends had assembled anticipating the big event. All at once the music began to play as Marsh waited for his darling Mary to appear. He thought his heart would burst with joy. As Mary began her slow walk down the aisle Marsh could hardly contain himself. As the pianos played "Here comes the bride", Marsh stood there singing in his heart, Here comes my bride.

As Mary reached his side, the minister uttered softly, let us pray, and then the ceremony began. After a brief pause the minister said to the young couple, join your right hands and say your vows to each other. When the vows were finished the minister turned to Marsh and asked, do you Marsh take this woman Mary to be your wedded wife, to have and to hold, forsaking all others? With no hesitation said, I do. Then he turned to Mary repeating the same question and Mary looking at Marsh said so lovingly, I do. Then the minister said, what God has joined together, let no man put asunder, I now pronounce you man and wife. Now you may kiss the bride.

When all the well wishers finished and congratulations were over, Marsh hurriedly whisked his bride to his waiting vehicle and away they went. Holding Mary close they hurriedly raced to Marsh's house to pick up things that they would be taking on their honeymoon. In the meantime Marsh's parents had rushed home to be able to present them a surprise wedding gift. As they entered the house they were met with Marsh's parents. His dad Narvelle said, your maw and I want to give our wedding gift to you now. Then taking an envelope from his lapel said, this contains keys and a deed to your new home and eighty acres of land. Marsh sat at awe as he explained I have twelve children, and that will be our gift to each of them as they leave our home. Upon hearing this and taking the envelope Marsh was ecstatic and began telling Mary, now when we get back we will have our very own home. Mary said how surprised she was and how totally happy she was about the gift from his maw and paw. After returning from the honeymoon which was wonderful, they began living and loving each other and making plans for their future. Mary remarked how she would want a big family and Marsh agreed saying, we will fill this big house with lots of love and what God will bless us with.

After a few months of wedded bliss Mary awoke one morning feeling a bit nauseated. She had never felt like this before and could not understand this feeling. She was trying to think if perhaps it was something she had eaten that was making her sick. As the feeling persisted every morning she told Marsh that she needed to go and talk to Maw. Upon telling and expressing her nausea, Maw promptly said, "Mary you are pregnant. You are going to have a baby!" Well with this news she hurried home to tell Marsh. Upon reaching home she happily told Marsh, honey guess what, Maw said I was pregnant and that was the reason for the morning sickness. With this thought Marsh was thrilled beyond words, not by her sickness but because we are going to have our little baby. First, he said, we must confirm that you are pregnant, then get you under a Doctor's care. As the weeks passed Mary could feel her body changing, and after a few months it was easy to see, indeed we are having an addition to our family.

As the months passed Mary was getting enormous in size and she knew her delivery would be soon. One night while she was sleeping so soundly she was suddenly awaken with a slight pain. She laid there still for a while as not to awaken Marsh. Soon however came another and another, each pain getting more intense. As the pain became almost unbearable she realized that she must tell Marsh, so she laid her hand on his shoulder and pressed saying softly, I think it is time for our baby to come.

This being the time that most babies were born at home with the assistance of a rural country doctor. So when Mary told him of her pain, he quickly got dressed and set out to get the doctor. With fears wailing up in him knowing he was leaving Mary alone, frantically drove as fast as he could, over bumpy dirt roads to the doctor's house. After telling him to come quickly Mary is in labor the doctor hurriedly followed Marsh home. After waiting for what seemed an eternity Mary heard the sounds of an automobile, then saw the headlights Mary said to herself, thank God they are here. Upon arriving, the doctor came in carrying his bag with all of his delivery supplies, and quickly began working with Mary to help her with this delivery. Being Mary's first the task would be more difficult, however being a country doctor he had done this many times, was very dedicated and really knew what he needed to do. After long hours and Marsh pacing, the little miracle had arrived. From the minute that Marsh heard the cry coming he came into the room. Staring at Mary to see if she was doing good as the doctor handed him the baby saying, here Marsh, this is your son. Taking the little new life in his arms, he said to Mary, we have a son, and loving her more than ever because she went to death's door in giving him this son. As Mary was made comfortable and the doctor attending her needs, Marsh held his little son wrapped in his blanket, staring down at him and seeing how perfect he was in every way. After a few days Marsh went for his sister and asked if she would come and help Mary until she was able to take care of herself and the baby. Back home and everything was going good, Mary said to Marsh it is time for us to name our son, so after going through several names they finally came up with the perfect name. We will name him Aubrey. He is so perfect no other name will do.

Mary and Marsh were so pleased with Aubrey that one day Mary told Marsh that she would like to have another baby so Aubrey would have someone to play with and not be reared alone. With a puzzled, but pleased look on his face, that is a great idea. So consequently they began planning for a second child. After all Mary had said that she wanted a large family. After a few months passed Mary announced to Marsh, our desires have come true, I am going to have another baby. So after the weeks, then months came for the delivery of our second child. They were familiar with the process as this had happened before so the second time would be easier on Mary and delivery time was much less. Of course, Marsh was by her side and finally the baby was born and the doctor handing him the baby saying, "Marsh here is your son." Marsh took him and looking at him carefully said "Yes, yes, another son, and he too is absolutely perfect." Mary was so proud of him and said I will always love my boys. Now by the end of the first day they had chosen a name. We will name him Heabert. Marsh jokingly said to Mary, "with this big farm we will need lots of boys." Needless to say Mary found herself pregnant again. This time came the third and once again another boy. After this birth Mary was not feeling good and being tired from the extra work she told him she needed some help, also I will choose the name for our third son. He also seemed to be a bit unhealthy so I will name him in honor of the doctor who delivered him. Marsh was very pleased with that so his name will be Matthew. Marsh told Mary there seems to be a pattern developing here for two years later a fourth baby arrived and it too was a boy. Mary said to Marsh do you have a good name picked out for our little boy and without hesitation he said, "Yes, I like Eddie". Mary said, "Yes that is such a sweet name, I love it, so say hello to little Eddie." Only one year and nine days, yes another baby boy. This in any other circumstances would be unusual, but with Marsh and Mary each child was truly a sweet blessing. Mary said then Albert it will be, with having five sons we will have a baseball team, not knowing that at that time Mary was pregnant again. So only seven months later another baby arrived and for number six this one would be, "oh yes" another boy. For some reason Marsh asked Mary, do you mind if I ask my maw if she will name our baby. Mary said that would be wonderful and she will be so proud. We don't see her very often because she is not feeling well most of the time. The next day Marsh went to visit her and asked her if she would name our little boy. She was so thrilled at being asked and said my very favorite name is Kenny, and with that she went straight to the baby's room picked him up and with a line of baby talk decided, yes this is baby Kenny. While visiting she remarked about what wonderful family they have and all the older boys are so helpful and well mannered. Then Marsh spoke up and said, I give Mary all the credit. She is a wonderful wife to me and a very good mama for our children. Mary told me after we married that she wanted a large family and this is what I want also, and we are still in love as much as the day we married. A year had passed and we were wanting another baby, and yes pregnant again. This time maybe a baby girl. As months passed Mary spoke to Marsh saying will you take the older boys to maw's house and go for the doctor. Marsh hurriedly gathered the boys together and told them, you are going to visit with your grand maw. They were so happy because she always had special things for each of them. After leaving the children with Mary's maw he hurriedly went for the doctor. By the time they arrived back Mary was completely ready for the delivery and Mary was having her seventh child. As the time grew near the excitement grew with anticipation of maybe a little girl. Upon the arrival however with red hair, big blue eyes, and such a perfect little baby. All of a sudden Mary started to cry and said, how could I be disappointed that he was not a girl. He is so strong and handsome. I will dearly love all of my seven boys.

She told Marsh, I have found the right name for him. I have one brother whose name is Rube and another one Ben, so I think the appropriate name is Reuben. Marsh said that is very clever and I think your brothers will be very pleased. So our seventh son will be Reuben. By this time Marsh was feeling so manly, yet so humble thinking to himself, how could one man be so lucky or fortunate. As night came and they had gone to bed Marsh asked Mary, at a later time would she be willing to try once more for that little girl. Mary agreed that she really wanted a daughter. Marsh then said I would want her to look just as pretty as you, so the plan began and Mary became pregnant again with her eighth child. The months that followed would be filled with excitement and anticipation of maybe having that baby girl. Finally the baby arrived and we have our daughter and Mary she will look just like you. Then Mary said I have already picked the name, I will name her Marsha in honor of you. Being aware that extra help would be needed Marsh hired a cook and a house keeper.

By this time Mary's maw begin to complain about Mary having so many children, which angered Marsh. He kindly reminded her that he and Mary were happy with our lives together and that was all that mattered. As a matter of fact Mary and I plan to have more. Maw being disgruntled with Marshes statement left saying, don't call on me for help because I will not be available. Mary said she was sorry maw felt that way, but she understood because she was already rearing her youngest sons children.

Marsh was known for being independent, taking care of his own and asking favors from no one.

Soon they were expanding their family with the arrival of another son. Seeing Brandon less aggressive than the others Mary said we need to work with him more. Soon I will need extra help with him alone. As you know Marsh we have another baby on the way.

So in a short time Mary was having another baby. This time another baby girl. Mary was so happy we will name her Windy. Now

Marsha will have a sister to play dolls with, and when they are older they can help me in the house and I will teach them to cook and sew.

As time went on there would be others. The next child entering this already large family would be Mary. Marsh said now we will name for you. She had red hair and blue eyes. Just looking at her now I know she will charm some gentleman some day. After this little girl Mary said I really like to have more children, for they are the light of my life. With that said she was pregnant again. With this message as usual he was pleased and this one will be in late December. This one we will call our Christmas present. As this baby arrived she was another little girl, Mary said now we have four girls, can you imagine all the silly giggles we will be hearing in the future. Then Marsh said what will we name her? Mary said I like Wanda, does that please you, and Marsh said that is beautiful and I'm sure she will be a beautiful girl.

Following Wanda Mary was getting older and feeling her family not complete so after discussing this with Marsh that no matter what others said we are not finished with our family. Now Mary and Marsh were trying to add more children. So soon Mary was getting sick in the morning and she knew that she was pregnant for the thirteenth time. This time seemed to be different. She began gaining weight rapidly and as time went on she had become enormous and people were saying, this must be twins, as if she needs twins. Yet all along Mary was saying no because she could feel only one movement. Marsh also had become concerned about her size. He paid special attention to the things she tried to do in the house, saying Mary please be careful and get your proper rest. Seeing that she was so uncomfortable he and the older children were trying to comfort her, also there was a precious family who lived near our farm. In that family was the mama, daddy and eight older children. Mary and Marsh had taught their own children to be kind and respectful to everyone. To the children they were known as Aunt Ida and Uncle Rufus. Marsh hired them to help, with Aunt Ida doing the housework in the kitchen Uncle helped Marsh in the blacksmith shop and on the farm. The shop did not take in much money. Marsh was able to pay his help and extend his services to other farmers and his black friends if they needed help.

Then came the time for Mary to deliver her baby as the labor pains had started. Mary promptly sent one of the boys to the field where he was working. While the child knew nothing of what was happening he knew by the urgency in his mamas voice he needed to go fast. Upon being told he stopped everything he was doing and rushed home. He told his oldest son Aubrey to take all the children to his Aunt Bertha's house and ask her if they could stay there for the night for mama was very sick.

Marsh wasted no time going for the doctor. Living about twenty five miles from the nearest hospital Mary had given birth to all of her children at home with the assistance of a country doctor. Upon arriving home with the doctor, Mary was really in pain. The doctor quickly brought his supplies in and started working with Mary. He could tell shortly that this one was going to be different with fear encompassing him, yet anxious for his baby to come, Marsh was scared and so sad for his sweet Mary to be suffering so much and wondering if she was going to be safe. An hour had passed and Mary's pain had intensified. As the doctor worked with her feverishly Marsh was beginning to panic. He was pacing back and forth past the bedroom door searching for a glance of Mary to see what was happening and also trying to see the doctor's face for some satisfaction. Seeing her and hearing her screams of agony he knew this one was much more difficult. He also noticed the perspiration and worried look on the doctors face. After working for hours feverishly the doctor man out and said this delivery can't be done here. I will give her something for pain and we must take her to the hospital. Marsh said I would like to make one step and pick up my sister Nellie to come with us. After talking to Nelly she graciously agreed to come.

On the way to the hospital Marsh was holding her hand and silently praying, "oh God, please help my little Mary make it through this delivery." They arrived at the hospital and was immediately given something for the pain and a short time later the baby was born. As Marsh and Nellie waited for the news of the arrival, the doctor entered the room. With much sadness and concern he announced, Mary we think is going to be fine but your baby has lost its struggle with life. Your baby boy weighted fifteen pounds and was virtually impossible to deliver alive. Marsh then asked if we could see Mary. They were then taken to her room and the three of them, Marsh, Mary and Nellie held each other and wept. Then Marsh spoke saying, Mary I am so sorry for all your pain and where all the baby angels are. With this the baby was wrapped in a blanket and handed to Nellie and they carried him in her arms to the family cemetary. On his monument Marsh had inscribed, Baby Murphy. He was given no name since he lost his life in child birth. Gone but not forgotten. The next few days were almost unbearable for the whole family, but as Marsh explained, life goes on for the rest of us, and we will return to as it was, because all of the other children will have to be cared for.

As for Wanda she would be Mary's baby the second time. After all she was only two and would love the cuddling once again.

After the loss of the little boy to a still birth Marsh and Mary would not accept that their family could stop here. They talked often about having more children, so one day Mary called Marsh into the bedroom and announced, we are having another baby, and in October we will be blessed with our next baby. It won't be like the dear one we lost, but this one will take away this sorrow feeling that I have from the one I lost.

So as I promised in mid October came the arrival of our baby boy. He was small but came into the world, kicking and screaming and truly letting everyone know he had arrived, and would occupy his place in this world. Mary and Marsh agreed to name him Leon. Once again Mary was so pleased with her little boy.

Now friends and family were whispering that Marsh and Mary really must be finished with their increasingly large family, but they were aall wrong. As Leon reached the age of two Mary was pregnant again. It was a cold winter, unlike most in the south, but Marsh was very diligent in keeping this big house warm and comfortable for Mary and the children. After a few months passed and spring had arrived Mary was getting things in order for the arrival of her next baby. In April as with the others at home she gave birth to this precious baby boy. Like a miracle he was born without a lot of pain and upon seeing him she began to cry. Then Marsh asked, my sweet Mary why the tears, are you in pain? Then she simply answered, no pain it's because he is so handsome. He had deep red curly hair, blue eyes and so calm. He is as though I ordered the perfect one. As he grew and developed he was always easy to care for. Being named for the doctor who delivered him, Gary so well suited him. However Mary's name for him was "precious little darling" because of his very sweet nature.

After a few years had passed and assuming their family was complete Mary began to be very sick. This continued for days and Mary felt that she could tell the reason for her feelings but Marsh was not believing another pregnancy. Early one morning as Mary was very sick Marsh said to her, get dressed I am taking you to see a doctor. As they entered the doctors office and was examined, the doctor said, Mrs. Mitchell you are simply pregnant again. According to your age this is a change of life baby. I can assure you this will be the last baby you will ever have, but he added with this one you must have the best of care if you want to carry for the full term and remain in good health for yourself. After getting a full set of orders they left for home. With the best of care you can carry this baby full term. As time grew near for what would be Mary's last baby anticipation grew. Would it be a little girl, another boy, would it be an easy birth, would it be a well formed healthy baby or something unknown. All these questions were nagging at Mary's heart. So early in June as the sun was rising labor pains began. Marsh being an early riser was already awake making his morning coffee. As the labor pains came closer Mary called out to Marsh saying it is time to go for the doctor. Upon hearing her he quickly rushed off to get the doctor. While her pains came closer she began to worry, when in a distance she could hear the sounds of the car and that meant the doctor and Marsh were near. After arriving the doctor wasted no time working with Mary in her last delivery. With her last hard pain and a vigorous push Mary heard the softly cry of her baby. As the doctor took the baby and laid it on Mary's stomach, he announced you have a baby girl. She was indeed a little girl, the smallest of any of the rest of Mary's children he had delivered. She had dark hair, hazel eyes and tiny feet and hands. After the doctor examined her he discovered that the fingers were slightly crooked, but assured Mary that in time they would be fine. He cautioned she would need special care and gave her a list of instructions. As Mary held her in her arms she marveled at how beautiful she was. Now Mary thought, what will I name this one. I think Ruby is a pretty name and as the Ruby is the most beautiful of all precious stones, so is my little girl. So Ruby is her name.

Now having related how this enormous family began I will journey back. And coming forward to the ways we coped in the happy times and challenges we faced. Daddy was strict with discipline with love but demanding respect, which he got. Mama was of a kind sweet nature and extended to all the love we needed. With this combination we were all stable and productive. Then came the news of a great depression. As daddy heard this he became totally disturbed. He knew the farm would be in part a great asset to raising his large family but it would not be easy. In the beginning things were going fine and was causing little or no problem for him. However as the depression raged on and all the neighbors were feeling the effects, daddy began to also to since many changes. He was getting the news of many businesses and banks shutting down he began to worry. Even his blacksmith shop was not as lucrative as it had been also his cotton crops and other marketable products were being affected. As like others he worked harder and harder to survive the devastation. It finally became so difficult he was forced to borrow money from the bank to be able to farm his land. To daddy this was a severe move but was necessary to be able to clothe and feed his family. At the end of the year he was notified that his property had gone for sale for the taxes he owed. He had no money and no job and no way to pay his taxes and we would surely lose our home. He checked on the time limit on how long he had to raise the money and was informed that the time had passed and the taxes had been paid by an old Uncle and he would take our home. We were given thirty days to vacate the house and land. Here we were mama, daddy and fifteen children with no place to live. Daddy being desperate assured mama that he would find a place for us to live, and we would survive. He immediately went searching for a vacant house to take his family. He returned in the late afternoon, saying I have found a vacant house and made arrangements to move into and also to use the adjacent land to farm and have a vegetable garden. Having borrowed money from the Federal Land Bank there would be enough left to buy our bare essentials to maintain until I can find some kind of work. In a few days as though a miracle daddy found a job working on a road project, and was able to move us to a better house and pay a small amount of rent. In the meantime the bank was petitioning daddy for the money he had borrowed, even though he had paid most of it back he had not been financially able to pay in full, the bank sued him for the balance, consequently ruining his credit. Here he was stripped of his honor and self esteem. Upon hearing about daddy's problems an old Uncle traveled from the State of Texas to visit him and help him financially. Seeing daddy was so worried Uncle Bob offered him a drink of whiskey saying this would give him a temporary relief from all his worries, but that was just the beginning of trouble for all of us. Daddy found that he liked the temporary relief and began drinking the alcohol more frequently. There after when he got his pay he would buy the bare essentials, then go by the local bootleggers house and buy moonshine whiskey. In most instances he would be drunk when he got home. Mama and the children never knew what mood he would be in. There would be times when he would imitate a black preacher, and then be mean to mama and all the children. Aubrey the oldest throughout his childhood had shown his remarkable intelligence. He had the desires of one day going to college. In grammar school and in high school his teachers remarked about his ability to learn and showed signs of his brilliance. His teachers took special interest in him. He spoke to them often about wanting to go to college after graduating from high school. With the depression still evident his teachers could see his dreams fade. With no money how would he be able to fray the expenses of going to college. With his interest in mind his teachers began to find work for him such as janitor, driving a school bus, working in the lunch room or various other things he could do to earn money to go to college. One day his chemistry teacher asked him if he would like to enter a Scholastic scholarship contest in Chemistry. The winner would be awarded a scholarship to the college of their choice. The contest covered East Mississippi and West Alabama. Upon hearing this he readily said, "yes" and if I win that would mean I could go to college. After all the preperations he was entered in the competition. Accompanying him to the hall where the competition was being held were some of his teachers. Students from near and far assembled and the competition began. Hours of work and stress was taking place. When all work had ended and papers turned in they were informed that they would no reveal the winner until the next day. On the way home one of the teachers asked him if he thought that he did well and he said, I hope so, however it was not a hard test. The following day the results were all tabulated and getting the call Aubrey had won. He during the award ceremony was given the scholarship but also a neck tie. While he thanked them graciously for the tie he was much happier for winning the scholarship. So in the fall after graduation he entered college.

To say the least it was not easy keeping his grades up and finding work to buy needed supplies and food.

Daddy and mama was so proud of him and while daddy was having a difficult time keeping up the rest of the family he would send him money, as much as he could, also from time to time other brothers would send him money. As soon as he could he joined the R.O.T.C. A military program and being an A. student graduated with honors and given the rank of 2nd Lieutenant.

The second son Hubert had express that he had no desirre for college or even grade school. Incidentally he dropped out of school and went to work for an uncle on his farm. It was hard work and he earned little money, but he learned so much about making a good living by tilling the soil and attending the livestock and many other chores on farm life. Consequently with time and dedication he knew what an asset he would be for everyone. He learned to buy and sell property, taking advantage of every opportunity and soon became self sustaining buying his own home and owning many valuable properties.

The third son Matthew always to be frail and unhealthy from the very beginning mama and daddy would pay special attention to his health issues. In those days he was not privileged to be under constant care of a doctor. Consequently he developed numerous boils, "commonly known as risings" about forty on his left arm. He developed a high fever and daddy rushed him to the doctor. Upon seeing him the doctor told daddy, "this is very serious and he must be hospitalized." After a few days he developed blood poison and became unconscious as nothing was helping him. After seeing him fighting for his life his arm would have to be amputated. While daddy was so afraid of losing his son he could not let his arm be amputated. As terrified as I am I have to say no. I refuse to let you amputate his arm. So the doctor told daddy the alternative is to remove the affected bone, coat it heavily with vaseline, wrap it tightly and pray. In a few days he became conscious, his fever subsided and he began recovering. After signs of fully recovering, an X-Ray was taken the doctor explained. This is truly a miracle, the bone has grown back. This one will go down in history as a medical miracle. The arm was left stiff in the elbow but his arm and life has been saved. Upon being discharged from the hospital he came back home and began thinking of things he could be useful doing.

He began woodworking as a hobby, and as he was enjoying this so much, he though, this is what I would like to do for an income.

He began to collect various wood products and make beautiful carvings. The more he worked, the more accomplished he became making amazing things. His best effort was carving parts and making a beautiful violin. With his mastery of the art this violin was truly a masterpiece. When finished and strings in place, it had the most beautiful sounds because he had taught himself to play. Our family was so proud of him and needless to say we enjoyed many evenings listening to him play.

The fourth son Eddie was a kind and lovable boy. As he grew up one could tell that he was the envy of everyone. He had red hair, blue eyes and very handsome. He was the idle of all the girls, but his generosity to mama and daddy was outstanding. He was the first to earn money and to send some to his brother Aubrey to help him stay in college. It seemed to him natural to want to help others. While we were still in the depression he left home and joined the C.C.C.'s. This was a government organization formed to let financially struggling people work on projects to earn money to survive. Then came Albert whose personality was very different from all the others. As he grew it was apparent that he was a bit selfish. Anything he owned was his and not shared with anyone. If he owned ten marbles they were strictly his. When he finished playing with them they were tucked away in his pocket. He never wasted anything but would find a good use for everything. He was thought of as being selfish, but it was soon learned that he would not be satisfied with just a normal existence, but wanted more. As he became a young man he was always figuring ways to earn money and save most of it. He soon began to be labeled as stingy but that didn't bother him, because he had a goal in mind. He often said, I will never be as poor as I was growing up.

Kenny, the sixth son was always the strange one. It was always difficult trying to figure out just what was on his mind. Even as a young child he was always trying to manipulate his playmates to gain advantage of them. Looking always for an angle to advance himself, not bothering about who got hurt in the process. He was eager to learn and worked well with his hands as he became and adult he was energetic and excelled at learning a trade like electric energy. Auto mechanic and home construction. He strived to meet his needs if it meant stepping on others to succeed.

Reuben was the seventh son. He would be in a special position, because seventh sons and no daughter was very unique. However he would develop into a warm and lovable son. As he grew into manhood he became very strong physically and happy. He could have, if he had chose so, been a prize fighter. All of his friends called him the gentle giant, but he had no desire to harm anyone. He too had joined the work group that his brother Eddie had saying this will teach me many skills that will benefit me later. He also said I can use the money for things I will need as I pursue a career.

Now the first daughter Marsha was so special and different from the seven older brothers. When she grew up and matured she was tall, thin and very beautiful. Her hair was light brown with a hint of blonde, her eyes were deep blue as the color of velvet violets. She became a daddy's girl as he would shield her from the wrath of seven older brothers. She was also clinging to mama for all of her needs. She was always willing to try to help mama with anything she was needed for.

Following Marsha was Brandon. The day he arrived daddy's friends had said, Marsh are you trying for your own baseball team? Well if he was this one did not fit in. Even when he was very young he seemed so dissatisfied, mischievous and lazy. Even when mama was near delivery of another baby Brandon refused to even try to walk. That is why mama's sister mane and wanted to take him home with her. When she saw him sitting on the floor crying she asked if she could take him home with her until mama could care for him.

Upon asking daddy he said no, that he loved all of his children and no one could separate us. From this mama felt a sense of relief and she and Aunt Flossie persuaded daddy to let her take him home with her. Daddy made it very clear that it would be only for a short time. Flossie had no children and could not have any so as weeks turned into months and then to years he remained there. Although there was no adoption she raised him as her very own.

Then came Windy, she would be the child that was a real challenge. She was a bit of plump, but very active. She had dark hair like mama, blue eyes and less than fair skin. Even though she was very healthy she would pretend to be sick or was hurting someplace just to get attention. She was always having anger moods and was reluctant to share or try to blend or play with other children. She constantly strived to get what she wanted one way or another.

After Wendy came Mary. She was a delight, very calm, even tempered and a very good little girl. She was like a breath of sunshine. She too had pretty red hair, blue eyes and pretty features. She was very good at entertaining herself and always cared for her appearance. And felt that her beauty could not be exceeded by anyone. She was ever so careful about hurting others and made friends easily. Everyone admired her good nature.

I Wanda being the twelfth child, as was told to me, I was a sweet adorable little girl. My appearance sole what was different than the other baby girls. I had blonde hair and green eyes, very calm and lovable. Since mama had such a difficult time with the thirteenth baby being a still birth, mama settled back and loving me as her baby a second time. As I grew I can remember as a loving mama keeping me close to her. I loved my mama so much and wanted to be just like her. As she would be sewing our clothes I would be by her side watching trying to learn from her. As I grew older she taught me how to cook, clean and do many things. She also taught me that no matter what you do make sure you do your best. I can remember hearing her say once, Wanda might be slow but whatever she does is always her best.

I can also remember how bad it was going through the depression and how mama and daddy worried so much about the children's needs. In my memory too was running to get on the school bus many times cold for the lack of a coat and warm clothing. Feeling ashamed of being shabbily dressed but a strong determination to do good.

At that time our government was trying to establish ways to help families in dire need as we were. Many people in our neighborhood would accept aid. As in the way all politics go, there was dishonesty in welfare programs and would be fully assisted in exchange for their votes. It was learned that mama's brothers gave in and was supplied all their needs and was paid ten dollars per month for their vote.

At one instance daddy was approached and offered the same, but being a proud and honest man he said no, and would no succumb to such dishonest behavior. He refused any type of welfare. We were indeed lacking in many ways, but daddy would make sure we had shoes to wear and adequate food on our table. Mama would make our clothes from flour sacks and fabric sacks that the animals feed came in. I also remember never having lunch money to eat in the lunch room at school. During the lunch period we would play and smell the food being served to those that were able to pay. We would always wait until school let out for the day, board the school bus and arriving home, run up the long driveway to our house, and eat what mama had cooked for us.

As daddy worked hard to provide for us, his drinking increased. By this time the older brothers grew tired of daddy drinking so much so one by one they left home to find work elsewhere. With Aubrey in college and Brandon still living with Aunt Flossie that left only seven of us at home. My oldest sister had grown and matured to the age to be noticing boys. She soon met who she thought was the right one, fell in love, married and left home. Being my big sister Marsha I missed her so much.

Just as the depression was showing signs of ending, came the news the Japanese had attacked Pearl Harbor. This was a horrible day for America and for parents who had sons. The draft board was established and all the young boys eighteen and older would be drafted into the Armed Services.

Our first to be drafted was Hubert. He was not educated and had never traveled more than fifty miles from home. It was so sad when he was called up for duty and boarded a greyhound bus. He knew no one or even where he was going. He along with many other young boys were sent to an army base, sworn in and trained vigorously, and after only six weeks of training, he and his batallion was sent to Germany.

By this time the Germans had joined the Japanese and declared war on the United States and we had found ourselves in a full fledged war.

The second brother to be drafted was Aubrey. It would not be as bad for him because he had graduated college in the R.O.T.C. The military branch and went to serve with the rank of 2nd Lieutenant, so he was more into training than battle. Later on however he was also sent to the war zone.

Next to go to the military was Eddie. The Japanese was trying to take Australia. He and his batallion were sent to the South Pacific. While Albert was hearing about his brothers fighting in ground combat he knew he did not want any part of that so before he was drafted into the Army he joined the Navy. Kenny was the fifth son to be drafted into the military, and last as Reuben reached the age of eighteen he was also drafted into the Army.

As it was now mama and daddy's sons, six of them serving in the military at the same time. Eventually each of them were sent overseas and in battle at the same time. As the war raged on daddy kept his ear to the radio listening to the war news and mama was sick with worry and praying. I can remember as a little girl hanging on to her dress one night as she went out on the prorch, lifted her arms up and prayed, "My God, My God, where are my boys tonight"?

I also remember her sister saying to her and I quote, "now Mary you have six fighting over there and you know they can't all come back." As I heard her say that, I thought to myself, how can she sound so cruel knowing how worried mama was and how desperately she wanted her boys back.

There were days when the postman would deliver a letter from one of the boys and as she read it a part of it would be cut out. This was because it might contain a location or plans about the next attack or any military secret. Nevertheless she wondered just what was he trying to tell me, also realizing if the enemy intercepted the letter it could reveal their location or a military plan that could put the entire squadron in immanent danger.

She knew already that Reuben was in General George S. Patton's third army, tank division. She had also learned that there had been bad weather and his tank had been disabled. He wrote her that he and three of his buddies were stranded in the tank. They could literally hear the German soldiers talking as they passed by. They had no idea that American soldiers were inside, otherwise they would have been killed. Reuben said they would have choked before they would have coughed or made a sound. After two days their division realized they were missing and came back for them.

Hubert too was in Germany fighting in close range combat. Living in foxholes they had dug, bitter cold snowy weather and hungry. He said we were about to lose the battle because the weather was so cloudy and gloomy the U.S. aircraft would not locate us to deliver food and much needed supplies. As one General later said that God has his hand on us because the next day the clouds moved out, the sun brightly shining and our forces flew in and delivered food and supplies. That battle was famously known as the Battle of the Bulge. While in another location Kenny's battalion was trying to figure out a way to cross the Rhine River. This battalion was commanded by General Dwight D. Eisenhower. Finally after extensive study he spoke to his men, asking who would volunteer to go on a suicide mission. The plan was to cross further up the river in a small boat and draw fire and in the meantime his battalion would cross the river further down. Kenny was one of the volunteers and as was quoted by Kenny, "we held on to the boat under the water while being fired on." It was really scary but we made it with no casualties. For this mission Kenny was awarded the Bronze Star.

In the meantime Albert was serving time in the Navy. He was trained for a short time and sent to the South Pacific. The Prime Minister of Australia had made an appeal for American assistance because the Japanese were trying to take Australia. The Americans were moved in as an importance to Australia's Naval bases. As Albert often remarked, the Japanese were fearless. They would fly suicide missions at our ships trying to sink us, but knowing they would surely die. However our ships were much more superior, and we would shoot them out of the air. General Douglas MacArthur ordered a massive buildup of American forces to combat the Japanese for the Pacific assault. At this time Eddie was sent for the buildup of troops and stationed at an Army base in Australia. He would never tell us of any bad times he had. He would just jokingly say he made friends with the kangaroos. Seeing no end of the war there came a desperate call for workers in the shipyards, ammunition and aircraft factories. My brother Matthew and daddy went to work in a shipyard. Matthew was classified as 4-f because of his stiff arm he was hired as a machinist. With six brothers in the war he felt his need to do his part. Daddy was not skilled for that kind of work but said he was willing to learn, and do anything he was needed for.

While working in the shipyard daddy managed to provide better for us at home. He said I can save money to buy some land and build us a house once again and own our home. After a long and devastating war with Japan and Germany it had finally ended. Our military had dropped the atomic bomb from the Enola Gay on Hiroshima and defeating Hitler and the German army with both surrendering. Upon hearing the war had ended, I remember mama saying, "I am so happy I could climb the wall backward", and I thank God all of my boys are coming home.

As time went on, one by one each of them were discharged from the military and finally coming home. I remember as each of them returned home we could see them at a distance walking up our long driveway. We all ran out to meet them and give them a big hug and welcome them home.

When these boys came home they seemed to have changed. We realized soon that they left home a boy and returned a man. While the war was tough on them, they brought back a tough look on life. Some worse than others, frequently going to bar room fights. To mama they were still her young boys, so their actions became a constant worry for her. They had been disciplined by daddy in younger years growing up but he said now he understands what the war had done to them and allowed for their actions now. So his solution for them was to agree to some of their actions and join them in playing cards and gambling with them to keep them home. This too was troubling to mama but she said nothing because she was so happy to have them back.

After telling the boys of the land he had bought he asked each of them if they would help him build a house because he was tired of paying rent. He also said I want my own home once again for my family and me. While working in the shipyard he was able to make the down payment on the land. However because of the bank loan that he made during the depression he was unable to finance the land in his name and was forced to put the deed in Kenny's name.

He was now back at home and had been given back his job working for the highway department. He continued making payments to the bank until the land was paid for in full. Then came the time to build the much needed house. All his sons would contribute money and labor. Daddy would go on the property, cut down trees and literally hewed by hand the cross ties that went under the house for the foundation. Soon the house was built far enough along that we could move in. It was truly a pleasure for us to live in our own home even not fully completed. I remember being able to look up and see the exposed rafters but we didn't mind because it was ours.

The house consisted of three bedrooms, kitchen and dining room, also a small front porch. We had for our heat a double fireplace. One served a bedroom and the other served the dining room. We had a deep well where we got our water. We used a bucket that was tied by a rope, let down in the well, filled with water and hoisted back up by hand and carried into the kitchen. Mama also cooked our food on a stove heated by stove wood. We lived in a rural community where electricity or running water was not available. We had no rest room inside so we used what was called an outhouse. An older brother jokingly remarked, "that we were so rich that we had carpet in our outhouse", and we liked it so well we carpeted all the way to the house.

Mama always cooked our meals before dark because we had only one lamp which was carried to each room that needed light. We were also very happy living in our new house because it was much nearer to a small store. Our school was only one mile away and we didn't have to ride the school bus but a short time. Mama and daddy made sure that we went to school and worked hard to make good grades. And that was their top priority. They expressed to us although we were poor we would not remain poor, and your education would be the answer. We would often be reminded of our older brother Aubrey who had become a success. Having finished college when he was drafted in the military he became a leader instead of a ground soldier. While in the military he met Kenneth his commanding officer and they became great friends. One day he told Aubrey that he would like for him to meet his sister. Seeing his commanding officer as getting old, grey hair, glasses and not a bit handsome. In his mind he was thinking this sister just might resemble her brother. Kenneth had told him that she was twenty five years old and hand no special friend at the time, but not to disappoint Kenneth he joined him for a visit and to meet his sister.

Upon arriving he had expected to see an old maid like, tall and skinny with horn rimmed glasses, but instead when Anna walked out she was breathtakingly beautiful. She had shoulder length hair, fair skin, beautiful blue eyes, tall and with an hourglass figure. Aubrey said for him it was truly love at first sight. After seeing each other constantly, he proposed, and in a big church wedding they were married. He was so proud of her he could hardly wait for his family to meet her. When he got leave he brought her home to meet us. We were also thrilled to meet her, not only because she was Aubrey's wife but she was so kind and had a lovable personality. She accepted us with open arms and we all loved her dearly.

After being discharged from the military Aubrey was determined to expand his knowledge, so they moved to Georgia where he entered Georgia Tech and got his masters degree in engineering. Anna got a job and worked to help with expenses. After living in Georgia for a while they decided to move to New Orleans where he went to work for the Corps of Engineers. It was there that they bought their first home.

Living there seemed to be just what they wanted from life. Being so successful was great but they began to think there was still something missing. One night while having dinner Anna brought up the subject of children. After a long discussion they both agreed that they wanted children, so now we plan to add to our happy home. After trying to get pregnant for months with no results, Anna went to see a doctor to find out why she could not conceive. She was told that there was no reason why she could not get pregnant. The doctor told her to ask Aubrey to come in and be checked. After seeing the doctor and going through the proper procedures it was discovered that Aubrey's sperm count was very low and that could be the problem. The doctor told them it could be either of them and they probably never would have children of their own. Anna being very disappointed decided to go to work for the government and Aubrey went to Tulane University as a professor teaching Civil Engineering.

Aubrey however was the one who led the way and was instrumental in showing his brothers and sisters what it meant to be educated and achieve success in life.

With my brother Hubert it was quite a different story. After the military he returned to what he had secured for himself. He continued to work his farm and save his money. He was not interested in socializing, but on certain occasions he would ask a girl to go to church with him. When he was in his high thirties he met a girl and became totally infatuated with her. She was too, very interested in him, so after a brief courtship they found themselves madly in love and married. It was not long after the marriage that she became pregnant. Oh yes, Hubert I am going to have a baby she joyfully announced. After the long months waiting she gave birth to little Lacy. As she grew Hubert thought that anything she did was so special and was the greatest thing a child could do. Soon there was another baby on the way. This time Hubert and Hannah would have a son born to them. Once again Hubert was boasting about what a fine son he had.

As his family increased he realized that they would need more income, so he went looking for a job. When he returned home he told Hannah that he had been hired and that he would be driving a truck. He had gone to a stockyard and would be driving a cattle truck. That would mean he would transport cattle from state to state and would also be away some nights, but agreed that they did need the money that he would bring in. He said however there would be times when he did not have a delivery and he would be home to help with the children and the farm. This arrangement was going good and then Hannah told him that she was going to have another baby. He assured her that he would be there for her and would take the time off when she needed him. As time passed and delivery time she gave birth to another baby girl. Hannah said this time we want a name to rhyme with Lacy so we will name her Stacy. As time went on they were successfully coping with a growing family, the farm and the truck driving job.

They were so happy and very satisfied with their little family, and thinking little Stacy would be the last, but Hannah had a secret waiting for him. As he reached home, picking up and loving each child Hannah slowly walked up to him and after the caress whispered to him. I have a surprise for you. With a puzzled look on his face said "what"? She answered with a half grin, I am pregnant again. He said in an unbelieving tone, "are you sure"? Yes she said, I went to see a doctor while you were gone, and another thing, I had an epileptic seizure. The doctor said I would be fine having this baby, but I must not have any more. Hubert said to her, rest assuredly this will be the last. You know that you can count on me for your every need. From then on he became the best husband and daddy one could ever be.

However at times he would be overwhelmed with Hannah constantly under the doctor's care, with the baby coming, the other three children to care for and the chores on the farm, but he kept reminding himself, I am a man, I am strong, this is my little family and I will cope and hold each of them dear to my heart.

As time passed and the time had come for the delivery Hubert was very worried. When the labor pains began Hubert rushed her to the hospital, the baby was ready to come. In a very short time the doctor came out and announced, you have a son, and Hannah is fine, it was an easy delivery and there were no problems.

As they were searching for a name Hannah said since this is our last we can use the last letter of the alphabet and name him Zachary. Hubert agreed, that is a perfect name. Hubert said, I have a perfect family, two daughters and two sons and also a perfect wife.

As the children grew and time came for them to start to school Hubert was there to make sure they were there everyday. He said he realized that not being educated was a hard life. Although he made it fine he wanted better for his own. He always took them to church and taught them right from wrong. He never stopped bragging on each of them and they were always taught with love and discipline.

After the war was over Matthew was still working at the shipyard, he was approached and ask if he would remain there. They were very satisfied with his skills and he was still needed. While living in a boarding house he had met the daughter of the owner, and they had become good friends. As it was she too had found him so very charming and the fascination began with both of them. Since Matthew was not familiar with a lot of the city she took the liberty of showing him the historic sights and recreational places where he had never been. This came from a casual friendship to a serious relationship to falling deeply in love. One day in a shy way she told her mother that Matthew and I are in love and he has asked me to marry him. I want to know if I have yours and daddy's blessing.

Her mother, with a pleased look on her face said yes darling, I have observed him for a long time and I think he is a fine man and he will make you a good husband.

Soon plans were made and in late summer they were married. As it was they wasted no time starting their family. So in the fall of the following year Irene gave birth to a son. Matthew was so happy with this little boy.

As expected they became the ideal family. As the years passed they became parents of four sons. This was the brother who had all the difficulty in his young life was now the envy of everyone. As his sons grew older he decided to leave the city and buy a place on an island. After purchasing a piece of land they would go there clearing the land to build the new house. It was understood he bought it for recreational purposes. So on his days off from work he would say to them, "come on boys let's go recreating". The boys were not happy about that work, but they had no choice in the matter. After all the plans were finalized and they were living there. They really enjoyed the boating, fishing, swimming, and all the other things that was available to them.

Irene's mother and daddy had run the boarding house since the war and was getting too old to maintain it, so they sold out and moved to the island where Matthew and his family lived. All of the family was pleased to have granny and pop come and live near them. Then one day Irene got a call saying Matthew was in a terrible accident. He sustained extensive injuries and was hospitalized for weeks. All the families were devastated. After all Matthew was the one that everyone depended on. Finally as he grew stronger and his injuries healed he was able to come home.

Back home we were going to school and doing our chores as was expected by mama and daddy. They made sure that we kept our grades up and we were not allowed to be lazy.

Windy and Marie, my older sisters were reaching their high teens and started dating and before long Windy had met a boy and told mama that she loved him and she was ready to get married and leave home. This too was a time mama's health was falling. She had been diagnosed with congestive heart failure and by doctors orders to refrain from any household duties. Consequently Marie and I assumed all the work around the house. I was assigned the cooking and cleaning and Marie was doing he outside work like milking the cows and feeding the farm animals. Marie and I shared washign the clothes and other things that needed to be done. Wendy had married and was taken far back in the rural countryside. She had become very unhappy living so far away and began telling Marie about her husbands brother. She would bring him to our house on occasions to see Marie. Before long Marie started dating him, and as was expected he talked her into marrying him.

By now I was in my mid teens and in high school. My main thought was to finish high school and go to college. I took extra work for credits to finish high school early and enter college. My oldest brother Aubrey seeing my determination for education and excellent grade average promised that he would pay for my college education. In the mean time I began dating a very handsome boy. I found myself thinking I was in love. After all he had declared his love for me and had asked me to marry him. At this he said he would not wait that long. So in my thinking he had already built a new house and furnished it for us and I would have running water, electricity and an inside bathroom, so I gave in and we got married. After a few months I found out that I was pregnant so after my first child was born I gave up my thoughts for college but in my mind I still intend to make my dream a reality. So "in my heart I said later".

After my brother Kenny was discharged from the military he went back to college and got a degree in electronics. During that time he met a girl, Millie and they dated for a short while, declared their love for each other and married. It was assumed he had told her that he owned a house and eighty acres of land, remembering that daddy had bought our land but because of bad credit he had put the deed in Kenny's name. So between Kenny and Millie the two of them they decided to take our home. So one day Kenny approached daddy and asked him to vacate the house. Being totally shocked daddy said no! I paid for this property and it is mine. With daddy's refusal to move Kenny left and angrily answered back, "we will see about that". So in a few days daddy was delivered a summons to appear in court to settle the matter of the ownership of our house. Not wanting to give up our home daddy hired an attorney to handle his case. Daddy had saved all of his receipts where he had paid for the property and took them to his attorney. He told his attorney that he had put the deed in Kenny's name, but he had paid for the place. The attorney knowing the deed was in Kenny's name but still took the retainer and also money for each visit to confer with him.

The court day arrived and mama and daddy took the three minor children went to court. The attorney asked mama if she would be willing to testify, and she told him, "I don't want to testify against Marsh but I can't testify against my son." The attorney told her, then I won't put you on the witness stand. Upon the opening of the court the Judge asked Kenny to plead his case, and while pleading his case he produced the deed that was in his name. Then the Judge asked daddy to plead his case and produce his evidence. All that daddy had to show was the receipts where he had paid for the property.

The Judge upon making his decision said, Kenny is holding the deed to the property and it is in his name. No on, even I, can't change a deed as it is written and notarized and signed and I have to rule that Kenny owns the property. Then the Judge asked daddy how he felt about moving his family, with all his crops planted and in the growing season and daddy replied, and I quote, "That's no way to treat a nigger." Then the Judge went on to say, "I will not Judge that Mr. Murphy pack up his family and move. He and his family can live there the rest of his life, and Kenny I hope you will never have another minutes peace the longest day you live for imposing this on your own daddy." During this case I was expecting my first child and my husband asked me not to attend the court procedures but if I had attended I would have voiced my opinion, that if daddy had put the deed in any other one of his children's name this would never have happened. As the days followed daddy seemed to have a broken spirit. He lost interest in taking care of things around the house as he had once done. He did supply the needs and was always happy when his other children visited.

I would visit as often as I could and take them things I thought they needed. When my first child was only one year old mama began to have heart problems. After consulting a doctor he informed her that she had congested heart failure. On occasions she would start smothering and have to be rushed to the hospital and once there they would relieve her by getting the excessive fluid from her lungs. She would remain weak but would be much better. After a few months later it happened again and was rushed to the hospital and they did the same procedure. Not long after the second attack she had a third. Once again she was rushed, getting a police escort, blowing the car horn, running red lights, and rushing as fast as they could but did not get there soon enough. She literally smothered to death. I was called to the hospital and told that mama had died. So heart broken I rushed down to be with daddy and my two minor brothers and baby sister. They asked me if I wanted to see her and I said yes, but to this day I wished I had not seen her. She was blue in the face and they had tied a strip of cloth around her head holding her mouth shut. My heart sunk when I thought, how horrible to literally smother to death. Sadness fell on me as never before as also the rest of the family. Daddy tried to be brave for the sake of the younger children but I knew how he was hurting. The next day I would see him wiping his eyes and he told us he had something in his eyes, but I knew he was weeping at the loss of his darling Mary.

This left daddy with two younger brothers Leon and Gary and my little sister Ruby who was only ten years old. While daddy did his best to be there for them they felt so alone without mama. My sister Windy living so far away in a desolate area persuaded her husband to let her bring her family to come and live with daddy and help care for the younger children and daddy. She having four children of her own was self serving and bossy created many problems, lending very little help to anyone, so it was decided that she take her family and move back to her own home which pleased everyone.

In the meantime little Ruby with daddy's help took on the responsibility of cooking and cleaning for everyone. Then came the weekend older brother Aubrey and Beth came back home for a visit, and seeing all the responsibility she was enduring ask daddy if they could take Ruby back to live with them. Daddy agreed, so to her delight she was able to live in the city and enjoy the luxury that they were able to afford for her.

This left the two boys Leon and Gary with daddy to fend for themselves. As daddy had always helped mama still knew how to cook and instructed the boys to pitch in and help. Daddy employed help on occasions and they learned to take care of themselves.

Finally as the years passed Leon graduated high school and joined the Navy. Gary continued to live with daddy until he graduated high school and went to live with his older brother Eddie who helped him get a job in construction. His first job would be driving a bulldozer making lots of money. He was soon driving a new car and later buying a little house. He was the talented one as far as music goes. He learned to pick a guitar and had a fabulous singing voice. He was drafted into the Army in peacetime but never liked it so after serving his due time was discharged and came back to his little home. After being home for a short while he went to work for an aircraft company and continued living alone. He dated many girls but never met one he wanted to settle down with. He continued to go out and socialize and enjoy his music. Anytime he went to a night club where there was live entertainment he would be called up to sing. He was also gifted in telling jokes and comedy routines. It was often said that he could have gone far in entertaining if he had been discovered or had the background financially. He fell in love with one special girl later in life but it didn't work out so he chose to live his life alone. He always said life was more peaceful that way. Daddy lived alone for years and had no interest in another woman. I lived nearer to him so I visited him often and he would come and visit me. I did everything I could do to supply his needs. I took him to the grocery store, doctor when needed and other times shopping or to visit family and friends.

One weekend he had gone visiting my brother Matthew in Mobile. He was enjoying his visit and someone suggested, let's play dominoes which he loved playing. Some of the others of our family were there also. While playing and having a great time he looked up as if to sneeze and fell from his chair. Seeing him in trouble breathing some one tried to revive him while the ambulance was called, but he had suffered a serious heart attack and died. This was really sad news for me. After losing mama, now daddy. I suddenly felt like an orphan.

As the weeks passed I felt so sad, but I too realized that I had my husband and three children, and this is the way life is. We must go on and take the good with the bad and always do our best. Then came the day Hubert was called to work. He was told that he would be driving a load of cattle to Tennessee, although he was a good driver while going down a huge mountain, the cattle shifted all to one side. The truck began shifting from side to side causing his truck to overturn down the mountain and he was killed. This was so devastating to our family and even more to Hannah and his young children. Although Hannah remained very sickly she did a marvelous job rearing families and are outstanding citizens, successful physically and financially. While Hubert was so proud of his family then, I'm sure he is looking down on them with more pride than ever.

Being from such a large family I stayed closely as each established their various vocations in life. Some were living near their birth while others far away. It was said that we were scattered from Maine to California, but we were always close in our hearts. Once a year there was always a family reunion and everyone came and brought their respective families. I was great to get together to laugh and talk, have lots of good food and remember the good old days.

As the years passed there would come a call that another brother or sister had passed away. Like the time we were called about Matthew. We had been so frightened when he was in the horrible accident, this call was so much worse. It was revealed to us that he was standing up working when he told one of his fellow workers that he was feeling very sick. Seeing him very pale and cold sweat on his face, they quickly seated him and called an ambulance, and like daddy he had died. This was so bad on Irene and his boys, and also her mother and dad because Matthew had become the rock and they all had learned they could depend on him.

Those of us who could go went to his funeral, and as he was a mason he was given a Masonic Funeral. It truly was a sad occasion and was the second of our brothers to depart our family. As it was with Eddie the sweet natured one had the desire to live alone. He did however give his younger brother Gary an opportunity to live with him and help him find work so he could be self-sufficient. He did however like the feeling of the effects of alcohol. For many years he abused himself in many ways as he over indulged in this habit. Having this addiction later in life he met this woman who liked the same thing and they decided to get married. To say the least this marriage was a merry-go-round.

She was hospitalized on one occasion when the doctor told her if she did not quit abusing alcohol it would surely kill her. So she promptly told him she would drink until she died. Not long after her statement to the doctor she was taken once again to the hospital very sick. Hearing this Leon, Eddie's brother went to visit him. While there his wife Nora died. Leon called me to tell me that Nora had quit drinking finally. I was so happy thinking maybe this would have an effect on Eddie, so I asked him how he knew that she had quit. He said as you knew the doctor told her if she didn't quit she would die and that is how I knew she had quit. We were never very close because of their life style but we offered Eddie all our sympathy as he and her family laid her to rest.

As time passed and he came back to reality he made the decision to stop drinking and return to a decent life. All his brothers and sisters were so happy and visited him often. He returned to being the lovable, giving, and caring person he once was. He later met a very nice lady and they adored each other. They dated for a long time. I remember them spending the night with me. She very boldly told me that Eddie had asked her to marry him and we are getting married, but I want separate bedrooms. I told her I agree because there is too much of that being done these days. They remained close and were making their wedding plans. Once again I was called and told that Eddie had died. He had come home from working, and as he walked up his steps fell backward with a massive heart attack. A neighbor saw him and tried to revive him but his death was so sudden no one could help.

He was brought home and we sadly buried him in the family cemetary. In my mind I was thinking losing three of my brothers and asking myself, who will be next?

Now Reuben had lived a somewhat loose life. After the war had ended he returned home. He gave in to drinking on certain occasions and too participated in bar room fights when he was under the influence of alcohol. Being the big strong individual he never lost any fights. This kind of activity really worried mama but she would only try to console him. On one occasion she same him literally jump through our screen door just to prove he was indestructible. This went on for a short time, but one day Aubrey suggested that he come to New Orleans and work for him. He worked there until it was complete, earned lots of money and came back home. At that time he told mama that his wild life was over and began going to church. This pleased mama and said my prayers have been answered just as they were when I prayed for him when he was in the war.

When he started going back to church he met this adorable girl Sally and they immediately fell for each other and before long the wedding bells were ringing for them. They were married in our small country church. He wasted no time getting a job and began planning to build a house for his darling Sally. They too agreed that they wanted a small family. So as time passed Sally gave birth to a baby girl. He announced to all his friends and family, I have the perfect wife and now I have a perfect little girl. They however would not stop there. They went on to have three sons. He worked harder and harder to be a good husband and earn a good living for his special family.

In a short time he had built the house of their dreams, and striving to earn money so that they could be properly educated. He continued to work doing double shifts at work thinking that he was indestructible, but one night he felt a bit sick while at work so with Sally's insistence went to see a doctor for a physical check-up. He came back saying the doctor said nothing was wrong, that I was in perfect health. Within a week while at home one morning he told Sally that his left arm was hurting and being concerned saying you need to go to the hospital. Sally said as she was driving him to the hospital. Sally said as she was driving him to the hospital he would raise his left arm over his head in excruciating pain. She finally reached the hospital and was carried to the emergency room. They told her to wait outside the room while they worked with him. In only a few minutes they came out and told her while he was on the examining table he raised straight up fell back down and was dead, that there was nothing they could do to save his life. With much grief for all of us, but his little family and Sally were alone and felt so hopeless. With much sadness but very brave Sally had him buried at the cemetary where they attended church. After getting things in order and grief eased somewhat Sally went to work not only to ease her pain but to earn money to continue to support the household and see that the children were cared for properly and educated. So as she worked and managed, she reared four of the best mannered and loving children one could ever wish for. As far as his oldest son, he is the image of his dad and completed a master's degree in Engineering, and the others were successful in other endeavors. I know how proud Reuben would have been seeing them grow and become so successful. I remarked to Sally one day, what a wonderful job you did with all your children. My brother Kenny worked long and tiring hours. He worked with electricity, belonging to the local union. He was sent out of town on various jobs. He and Kathy were proud parents. He built a house on the same property they never discussed it again. Daddy had been badly hurt by him, he felt in his heart he is my son and I forgive him. So before daddy died they had talked and made peace with each other. Living so close Kenny began to assist daddy in things he needed him for. However when daddy died Kenny came straight to our house and got daddy's strong box which held all of his records. Kenny was totally interested in educating all of his children. When his two oldest sons were in college, doing great and graduating together in the fall, they had been home in the summer.

The second son had gone out with some friends partying and as morning came his mom checked his room and he was not there. She and Kenny began to worry and went out to look for him. Soon they were stopped by the law officials and asked if Johnny Murphy was their son. They said yes and we are concerned because he didn't come home last night and we are looking for him. They said, look no further, he and his brother-in-law both were found dead on the railroad track. Kathy screamed, My God No, not my son. Kenny's heart sank as he began questioning them. Who would do this and why? He was told we will have to investigate and who ever did this will be brought to justice.

The investigation went on for weeks with no arrests. Soon Kenny and Cathy hired a private investigator and worked with him for months. Costing them a small fortune and no success. This was one murder that to this date has never been solved. From that day forward Kenny was never the same. Johnny's room has remained the same way he left it and his car was secured, never to be driven by anyone again. After that Kenny started having heart trouble and was hospitalized many times. He finally gave up the fight and died. So sad for me losing another brother but in my heart I'm thinking just how bad it would be losing your child. Kathy today is suffering from Alzheimer's and hardly knows her own name. She told me before she became so sick that the property they went to court for would be evenly split between her four remaining children. Today all of her children are caring for their mom, each of them one week of each month.

It seemed that sadness is overshadowing my life but somehow this is how we live and have the courage to withstand. My brother Aubrey also had a good and spectacular time, but also had his burdens to bare. In the beginning he and Anna were the ideal couple. They were making lots of money getting many friends. Constantly partying and going out with friends to places of entertainment and bars. Soon as this continued Anna started to frequent bars alone. This became a real problem and she couldn't seem to control her drinking. She soon started going out alone and driving back home at night drunk. Aubrey in desperation called her family. Upon hearing this her brother Kenneth and sister's Mary and Francis. And with Aubrey's help put her in a dry out center.

After a few months it was decided by the authorities that she was cured and could be discharged. When she was free to go Aubrey went to the center, picked her up, and took her to a nice restaurant for a good meal. As the waiter came for their order, to Aubrey's disappointment she ordered a double Martini.

He later related to her family how much money the center had charged him and it was all in vain. She had not been cured at all and when they were back home she was worse than before. So as she continued things went bad for both of them. Soon they were divorced and he became reunited with a high school friend. They soon became more than friends and decided to get married. Later it seemed not as much love as it was a convenience. Needless to say they soon divorced.

Aubrey was never one to be alone so while attending a football game he met a much younger girl. They had a whirlwind courtship and she being an opportunist agreed to marry him. After being with her for a short time he really got to know her for what she was. She had two little girls which he readily accepted because he had always wanted children. He always made concessions for her bad behavior, but when he found out that she was a cleptomaniac and had been stealing things from their friends he said enough is enough so he divorced her.

After that he retired and returned to his home state. When never wanting to be alone he once again met this older woman and started seeing her on a regular basis. He vowed at this time never to marry again.

One night while staying over night with her he woke up and could not get out of bed. He could not move his left arm or left leg. She quickly called an ambulance and he was taken to the hospital and was readily diagnosed as having suffered a stroke. Our family brought him home and helped him get the best of care and assisted him in getting therapy sessions, but he was never able to gain any movement back on the left side.

Finally feeling so defeated he asked us to take him to a nursing facility where there would be nurses to care for him properly. I visited him every day and as luck would be the facility was across the street from my house. I could put a steak on the grill and get it to him before it got cold. I would take him a crayfish, which he loved, sit outside and peel them for him. That was one of his favorite foods.

I can remember when a storm was coming up one day, so I called him and told him of the pending bad weather and I could not come and his remark was, "does your car leak", and chuckled in the phone. He always had a sense of humor even as sick as he was.

After months of being paralyzed on the left side, numerous trips to the hospital and in general bad health, he was getting so frail and miserable. One night I was called and told that his battle was over. Even though I comforted him and visited him he was alone one night and died in his sleep. He had previously given me his power-of-attorney, so I was at liberty to take care of the arrangements and settle his estate with his living brothers and sisters. He had always been my favorite brother and I was deeply hurt with his passing.

Now I come back to reveal the times and trials of Albert. After being discharged from the Navy he came back home and eagerly sought employment. While in the Navy his pay was very little, but he managed to save some and always wanted more. He bought a small house and moved in and batched. He continued to live on the bare minimum and continued saving all the money he could. Just on the jovial side, one day he was offered a cold soft drink, and he answered, "No thanks, but I will take the money." He continued to work and save.

One day the opportunity came to purchase a larger and more valuable piece of property. He was finally beginning to wear the title of a success story. Now having an attractive bank account and valuable properties he was gaining respect and favor in the community.

As word spread about his ambition a pretty young girl named Arlene started coming by his house and befriending him. Soon they became more than good friends and fell deeply in love and married. He continued to work and save, however she let him know that he could be as frugal as he chose, but their needs would be met. With that statement from her he agreed. After that they started to add to their family right away.

First to enter the family was a little girl, then a son was born. With his family increasing so rapidly he realized his pay scale in his area was to low so he moved his family to Atlanta and found a much better job working for Lockheed Aircraft. This location and job opportunities were much better since they wanted more children. Soon there was another son born.

After the third child arrived for some reason there seemed to be a problem developing. It soon became so serious they decided to become separated. While the children remained at home with him Arlene left and went to work as a waitress and was enjoying her freedom from responsibility.

She started going out with other men, but in her heart she still loved Albert. So one day she called him and said that she wanted to come home, and still loving her he told her to come home, that he and the children had really missed her. Not longer after she came home she announced that she was pregnant. Then the question arose about who could be the daddy. Nevertheless she remained home and gave birth to the third little boy.

Albert never nagged or questioned her but loved him just as he did the others. With all the nosy and suspicious people, they would ask about the little boy and he would just laugh and say, it's fine I have the best three out of four not giving them any satisfaction for their cruelty.

In his heart he was happy having his family back together. He continued working and would tease fellow workers about how he liked golf. They would say, man I didn't know you played golf, then he would reply, I don't but when some of the fellow workers want a day off to play golf they will let me work in their place. This was just Albert, always trying to be successful. He continued working for Lockheed Aircraft and was nearing retirement and Arlene announced she was going to have another baby. He being so thrilled told his fellow workers, and one joker told him, man I think someone has got it in for you. Being the good natured person he was laughed along with them. After working many years and managing his money he retired and bought a funeral home in Atlanta. Even though he was getting older he was managing the funeral home. It was not hard.

After a few years he sold the funeral home and moved back home. By this time his youngest son was ready for college and wanted to go to Clemson in South Carolina. So no wanting to pay out-of-state tuition he once again moved to South Carolina and brought a big beautiful house. After living there for only a short time Arlene grew unhappy and once again ask for a separation. He then came back home and began living alone. He began buying other properties, renting them and once again making more money. On day to his surprise his son Charlie had left his wife and three children and came to live with him. He had gotten himself deep in debt and it was clear that he needed financial help. During that time living with Albert he divorced his wife. Then met a girl and remarried. They both lived with Albert after they married. One day Albert became very sick and was taken to the hospital and upon examining him was diagnosed as having lung cancer. Being old at this time his son Charlie insisted that he should give him his power-of-attorney. Albert refused at first but gave in when his son told him if he had money medicare wouldn't pay for his hospital bills.

After Charlie got his power-of-attorney he placed his dad Albert in a care center for the terminally ill. However when I went to see him he was able to go home but is son refused to take him home, so I consulted the management and asked them if I could take him to my house for visits and was told I would have to get permission from Charlie, his son, because he had his power-of-attorney and he was in charge of his daddy. Finally I got permission and took him to my house for lengthy visits.

One day when Albert was talking to a friend he asked why he sold a certain piece of property and Albert said, I have no sold any property. He said yes you have, I know who bought it and it has been recorded at the court house. Then Albert called me and asked if I would take him to the courthouse. Upon arriving there he was told it was said to me, will you take me to my bank because Charlie is a signer on my accounts. He upon checking found that Charlie had taken large amounts of money out and on many occasions. My brother Albert was so upset and said, "That is stealing", he has taken my money and sold my property without my permission. Then he said he probably opened a private account, took my money so Arlene and other brothers and sister would be left out. Albert told me if he ever had a favorite child of the five children ti would have been Charlie. Then he told me if I had not taken him to the court house and the bank he would never have known that he could have done this to him. At that time I told him, never give anyone your power-of-attorney simply because money makes a fool of people. Later on Charlie put him in a nursing home. Even though he had lung cancer and should have been treated and cared for in a hospital. He still did not bother with his needs and seldom visited him.

I visited him every day at lunch time so I could help him eat his lunch. He became weaker every day as he would cry and say, "I just want to go home". Will you tell my youngest son to come and get me. I got in touch with Casey and Arlene and told them that he couldn't live long, so they came and visited him. It was so sad seeing him like this and while he and Arlene had seperated they had never gotten a divorce. He had given her the house in South Carolina and he lived in the old home place. I believed they still loved each other. The strange things was when she came to see him and he had gotten so weak she was the only one he would let feed him. Shortly after their visit one night he died in the nursing home.

In my fury I told all of his family, with lung cancer he should have been in a hospital, not a nursing home. This too was such a sad feeling for me losing another brother. We buring him in the cemetary where mama, daddy and the other departed ones were buried. As I am now thinking of my sister Marsha, as a little girl I always depended on her and loved her. I thought she was so pretty and as my big sister paid special attention to me. I can remember how sad I was when she married and left home. She moved far away and we seldom to to see her. She started her family right away and her husband moved her in with his family because he was too lazy to work and support her. Finally as the years passed and having three children his family made him take his family and move to their own place. With that Marsha was totally stressed out. So one day mama got a letter begging her to come and help her because she was going to have her fourth child and needed her badly. With that mama took my baby sister Ruby and rode on a Greyhound bus to Waynesboro to help her. Arriving there mama was so devastated. She was living in a shack not fit for human beings to live in with barely enough to eat. The children were shabbily dressed and looked malnourished. Her husband James making all kinds of excuses, that he had lost his job, but was starting another one on Monday working at a saw mill. After staying until the baby came and she was able to travel she and the children came home with mama. Daddy said although we don't have much I have always found a away to care for my own and you are one of us. So she continued to stay with mama and daddy for a few months.

Then one day her husbands mama came and told her that her son wanted her and the children to come home. So she packed all their things and went back home. He was very glad to have her back and to see the children, but still no job. Marsha quickly told him if he did not get work she would, that they had children and they had to be fed and clothed, so when he made no move to go to work she kept her word. Marshal went to work in a factory while he laid in bed all day and read Love Magazines. Soon she could see that he was neglecting the children so she hired a maid to care for the children while she was at work.

One day she was called home, that there had been trouble there. Upon arriving home she saw two policemen arresting her husband, putting handcuffs on him. She quickly asked "what is going on here", and they replied, your husband has raped your maid. She thought in her mind, "what can I do now, he has been arrested and put in jail".

She continued to work until his trial. When the trial was over he was sentenced to six years in prison. After pleading to the courts that she had four children and no home and was unable to care for them and support them and instead of helping her they were sent to an orphanage. At that time she was so devastated and I asked her to come and stay at our house until she could find work and take care of herself.

During the time he was serving his sentence in prison she found out that she could secure a divorce without him signing so she hired an attorney and filed for and got a divorce. She had no automobile, nor did she drive so I took her to see the children often. It was so heart-breaking each time she had to leave them. Most times she would cry all the way home. After working for a few years she met and married again, thinking she could go and get her children, but while living with him she found him to be an alcoholic and she knew she could not bring them into a situation like that. After a few years of abusing his body he died. With what he left her, which was very little, and what she could earn, she was able to buy a small house. By this time her oldest son became of age and was able to leave the orphanage. He lived with her for a short time, met a girl, married and left home. At that time she proved that she could support the other children so she was allowed to bring them home.

As the two girls finished high school they both married at a very young age and her youngest son became a policeman. Shortly after all the children had settled down to a happy life she felt a sense of satisfaction. She visited me and the children often and expressed that this was the happiest time of her life. As she was beginning to age a little she called me one day saying she was having pain under her rib cage and ask me if I would take her to see a doctor. Upon seeing him he told her he could feel a tumor and it was in a bad place. So he sent her to a specialist and after X-rays and the

47

examination he told her that she had pancreatic cancer. He told her there was a chance with surgery and I was with her. I will never forget the look in her eyes when she asked me, "did they get it"? I said, "no but they said with chemotherapy they think they could shrink it". After that chemotherapy was so horrible. It was not shrinking it but was making her deathly sick. Finally the pain was so severe that she was hospitalized and had to have sedatives to relieve the pain. This went on for six months when she would be sent back to the hospital when she would be sent back to the hospital when she could not tolerate the pain. I was with her every day and when her pain would get unbearable I would go to the nurses station and ask for something for pain. Then came the day she was rolling all over the bed with pain and I told the nurse "you have got to give her a shot to kill this pain." Finally the nurse came in and gave her the shot and she ask, "did I get it, did I get it?" I told her yes, yes, you did. Then she laid back, rolled her eyes back and she was gone. As hurt as I was losing her it was a relief to see her free from all that pain.

Following her was Brandon. He being brought up by his Aunt, had a very privileged life. He felt the real need for a good education. After graduation he went to work for the railroad. There he had a very good salary and the retirement was going to be good. While working there the Korean conflict broke out and he was drafted in the military and sent to an Army base, trained and sent to Korea. He was not there long because the conflict was ended. He suffered no injuries he still had to serve his four year term.

After being discharged he met a beautiful girl named Joyce. They fell in love and had a beautiful wedding and a wonderful honeymoon. They were so happy for a few years but she often showed how tempermental she was and was accustomed to getting her way, and also Brandon was self-centered himself.

Soon the clashes began and too he found out that he had married a wife for himself and others one also. While he was at work she was being unfaithful to him. One day he arrived home early and found her having an affair with his cousin, so he said enough is enough. After that he filed for a divorce and it was agreed on by both.

I can recall the time when he came to my house so broken hearted and talked to me. Perhaps I gave him the wrong advice, but I told him the best way to get over one, is to get another one. His answer to that was, "The next time I marry I will get one so ugly no one will have anything to do with her". So he moved back to his Aunt's house. Upon hearing that he was divorced and back home a girl who lived nearby started coming by his house almost every day. They soon started dating and soon were married. To say the least he kept his word. She was not like the beauty that he had married before.

They immediately began their family and he became a good husband and daddy to their four children. He made certain that they got a quality education and never let them lack for anything they needed.

Once again as he grew older, like the others he became stricken with heart problems. He stayed under a doctors care for years doing everything he was instructed to do. Finally he had a severe heart attack, stayed in the hospital for days but died with all his beloved family around him. My sister Windy was a different story. She had always pretended to be sick while living at home and it continued throughout her life. Although she had a hard life, living on the bare necessities she was able to give birth to four children. Her husband was a hard working little man who lived under her dominate hand. She got her way by playing sick or use her religion.

Then there were times she would be ultra sweet which they enjoyed so much that she could dominate. However they managed to educate two of them which were very successful, one became very ill and died in early adulthood. The other was the problem child. In her heart she tried to be a good mama to her children by cooking big meals, taking care of their needs and always taking them to church. Her husband was always devoted to her as she was to him. When he died she was broken hearted, sad and alone.

Her children came to visit her often and helped her emotionally and financially. The problem son remained at home with her, and the others seeing the bad time she was having with him and she was too old to cope. After discussing her situation they chose to put her in a nursing home.

My younger brother and I visited her often. She seemed very satisfied, with no responsibility, food served to her and free from the mental stress from her wayward son. She always greeted us with a smile. As we talked about old times, they told us at the home that she was getting dementia and soon afterwards she died in the nursing home. As I am looking back she was not a problem sister but her ways were different, and I loved her and still miss her.

Now my sister Mona is difficult to write about because we were so close growing up. When mama became so sick we shared all the chores. She was two years older than I and had failed a grade in grammar school so we were in the same grade and we had all of our classes together. We were on the same basketball team, "even though she was a better player". We still enjoyed the trips and playing together. I was engaged to be married but certainly in no hurry. In that same year she married and moved far back in the country near Windy, having married her husbands brother. Things were not easy for her either. Her husband had a twin brother who lived with them. She worked very hard keeping the house clean, cooking and was expected to work in the fields helping grow crops which she did.

She also gave birth to three children that had to be cared for and yet made no demands for herself. As the children grew older it seemed that her husband and his brother were always conspiring against her and even brainwashing them. He too was a man who did no want to get a job and bring in money to supply their needs. He depended on his small farm for their living. As the children were in grammar school she could see their needs so she went to work in a bakery. While he enjoyed the fruits of her labor he became obsessively jealous of her talking to customers.

One night he came to the store where she was working and watched from outside as she was being friendly and laughing with her customers. When she got hom from work he started cursing her and accusing her of being unfaithful to him. She tried to tell him that she was told to be nice and friendly to the customers. Then he threw her across the bed and started beating her. Finally when she could get away from him, she came to my house crying all bloody and so upset. After that she stayed at my house but he would not let her see the children and continued brainwashing the children against her.

After she could not live like that any longer she filed for a divorce. By the time the court case came up he had threatened the children and made them testify for him. He told them that if they didn't stand with him on the witness stand he would come at night and kill all of them. The youngest son told his mom, "I don't want to go against you, but I've got to."

Consequently when court was in session all three of the children said they wanted to live with him, so the Judge ruled that he could keep possession of the house and the children would live with him. The house that they lived in was purchased by her. She had borrowed the money for the down payment. We as a family were so disappointed for her and expressed, what a miscarriage of justice. She lived with me for a few months and finally was able to buy another house. As time passed and the children had become of a legal age they visited her often.

One day while she was working at the bakery she became very sick. I was out of town so my husband picked her up and took her to the hospital. She continued to be so nauseated and could not stop vomiting. After treating her and running various test she was diagnosed as having pancreatic cancer. She was told that she would live about six months and was advised to take chemotherapy, and after seeing her sister Marsha suffer the way she did she said no. She said she would live as normally as she could but if surgery was an option she would agree to having surgery. I along with other members of our family took her to a cancer specialist center. She had the surgery but we were told that they could not help her because the cancer had spread to other parts of her body.

We carried her back home and members of our family took turns caring for her. As her pain became so severe, we took her back to the hospital, and as the doctor predicted she lived about six months.

I, along with her daughter was with her when she died. I was so depressed at losing her, thinking of all the things we did together and also remember her saying when she was so sick. She would be crying, saying, I don't want to die and leave my children and grandchildren because I love them so. Her memory will be with me and the sweetness she left will always remain.

I now will relate the time I spent with my younger brother Leon. He was born after mama gave birth to the baby that died at birth. Even though he was small in statue he was very big in intelligence. Even though I was older we spent much of our time competing in many endeavors. By the time he graduated high school I was married and had started my family. In the summer after he graduated he came and lived with us a short time. Even though he was a candidate for college he had no money so he chose to go into the Navy. After being in the military in peacetime for four years he decided he liked being there and re-enlisted for two more years. While serving he met an adorable girl named Betsy. She liked the traveling that they did so being together constantly they knew they were meant for each other so they married. She was a registered nurse and he had ranked very fast. The life in the military was great. Shortly after marriage she became pregnant. They were so happy that they were having a baby they decided that when his time was up he would get out of the navy and come back home. He moved to another city and became a real estate agent. He became so successful he applied for a broker's license and opened his own real estate business. He had bought a small house and the baby had arrived so he felt the need to expand his business so he hired more agents. Seeing his business was going to great he was able to build the house of their dreams. Betsy was also working as a registered nurse and making a good salary and he added even more agents. At this time he had eighteen agents working for him. Things were really going great.

Then one day Betsy came to his office and told him to "hang on to your seat, we are having another baby". He was so excited and said this is great, I am making enough money you don't have to worry or go back to work. After her time was up she gave birth to a new baby girl. They were so happy with their new home and their two little girls.

Then one day while at work he suffered a severe heart attack. He was rushed to the hospital and it was recommended that he undergo bypass heart surgery. I came there and stayed with him through the surgery. While he was recovering he called one of his agents and asked him to take care of his office while he was out, but his recovery was such a long time and the business was failing he was forced to close it. Consequently the money stopped coming in.

He expressed one day that while he was doing so well he sat in his office, only went out to eat, not getting any exercise and his veins filled with cholestrol causing his heart attack. After recovering from the surgery the doctor said he could not go back to work because of the stress so he was put on disability status. After that Betsy became disgruntled about being the only one working. I guess what my daddy always said, "a woman will forgive anything but giving out of money".

So after a short while she persuaded both girls to stand with her, filed for a divorce and the girls testified on her behalf. She asked that he be made to move out of the house giving her full possession. With his illness he had lost so much weight he weighed about one hundred pounds and was unable to work and looked very frail. The judge said to her, I will not judge that this man be evicted from his home and he will have half interest in the house ans long as he lives. So she takes the girls, buys another house, leaving him alone.

I would visit him and take him things that I thought he needed. My other brother, that was younger, and I would go and take him places he liked to go and would spend the night with him, which he loved. I always cleaned his house and made him as comfortable as I could. One day Betsy called me and said she had gone over to check something at the house and said Leon is gone, he died in his sleep. His youngest daughter had become and Episcopal priest and when we had him buried his daughter preached his funeral.

Now remembering the sweetness of Gary. He chose always to live alone. In his younger days he found what he thought be the love of his life. Her name was Francis. He fell madly in love and as things didn't work out for them he went into a slight depression. He came to our house after the breakup and I really thought he had lost control. He didn't talk much but when he did nothing he said was rational. We tried to comfort him and agree with him. He did nothing but sleep for days. Finally as the days passed we could see reality come back. Finally he wanted to go back home and we felt that he could. So we took him back home.

An older brother came and insisted that he go home with him and he would help him find work and be independent. I always thought that was his time to mature and become a man as that was what he did. He became the happy-go-lucky person and didn't want to be bothered with other peoples problems. Although he was sweet natured and wanted to be around happy people and make them laugh. He visited me often and I would go to his house and as usual I would clean his house which he liked even though I on occasion misplaced things.

In later years he developed heart disease. I would accompany him for his appointments or minor surgeries. On one occasion he was sent to another city to have major surgery. My son and I took him there and he was told he had a fifty percent survival. He answered saying, I have a one hundred percent demise if I don't so let's do it. So as miracles go he had a quick recovery. After returning home and he began seeing his regular doctor, he called me aside and told me that he would not live six months with his heart condition.

Once again he defied all odds. Two years later he was still fine with his heart problem. However later on he began to be nauseated and could not eat certain things without getting sick. When he told me this I said we need to find out what is wrong, so we are on our way back to see a doctor. After seeing a doctor and all the various tests were confirmed it was determined that he had cancer of the stomach. How very devastating for both of us to hear. He was given the choice of radiation, chemotherapy, or surgery. He told the doctor he did not want radiation or chemotherapy but he would go for surgery. When the doctor consulted his heart specialist he was informed that he could not have surgery because he would not live through it. Consequently his heart was too weak to withstand it.

After the decisions were made Gary said I will remain as I am and have so me quality of life as long as I live. Then he said to the doctor will you keep me from pain. The doctor said I promise you will be free from pain. Well from then on things went bad for him. It had to be bad living at home alone just waiting to die, so I insisted that he come to my house and not be alone. He told me he just wanted to stay at home, that he liked being by himself, out in the country and no one bothering him. I said alright but don't hesitate to call me when you need anything. From then on he would call me to take him to see his doctor or for groceries. He would say if you can come and pick me up I don't have city drivers license, "jokingly", he did but he was getting to weak to drive.

One day he called me and told me that he wanted to come to my house because he was getting too weak to walk up his steps to get in his house, so I immediately went and brought him to my house. At this time my little sister was visiting me from California and she was happy to have him join us. As she said, this is a real good memory for us, we are here together, the last three of us that is still living.

As the days followed she and I took very good care of him. He also had health care nurses coming to my house checking on him. Then late one evening as I was checking on him I could see in his eyes he was slipping away. I kissed him on the forehead and said I love you and you are doing good. He said back to me, "it's like the little dog that got his tail cut off, it won't be long now."

With that I rushed to the phone and called the health care nurse and she came immediately. She was with him a short while, then she came and told us to come in the room that he was dying. So my sister Ruby and I stood at the foot of his bed and quoted the Lord's prayer as he passed on to be with Jesus, no pain or any struggles, just peacefully.

Now with all the sadness in my heart it is overwhelming, and this brings me to my title "And Then There Were Two". As I am coming to the present Ruby and I still remain. We will still carry on as troopers in what has been a beautiful struggling journey.

As Ruby has had her difficulties, losing her mama at the age of ten, then being cared for and educated with help and guidance from our brother Aubrey she has led quite a different but successful existence. While living in New Orleans she met and fell in love with Donald. He was an officer in the Navy and falling deeply in love with her told her, "Marry me and I will show you the world". She said yes and he gave her a beautiful diamond ring. Then as time went on scared and unhappy about her decision and decided that marriage was not for her and gave the ring back. While being alone she began to think that she missed him more than she ever imagined she would, so she called him and said how sorry she was about the decision to give the ring back, and said if you will still have me, will you marry me? He said he thought about saying no but realizing how he still loved her and came back. Then without hesitating they flew to Las Vegas and was married in the Chapel there. Before long she found out that she was pregnant. During teat time she began traveling with him wherever he was stationed. After a few months the baby was a little girl and they were deliriously happy. They had rented an apartment and life was wonderful. It was near Christmas and she had taken the baby who was eighteen months old, in her stroller and did some extensive shopping. Being tired she put the baby in her bed and she and Donald went to bed as usual.

The next morning they noticed the baby had not awakened making jovial baby noises as usual so they went to check on her. She was lying on her stomach and Donald picked her up and her little face was blue and she was not breathing. She had died in her sleep, that was that the doctor called a crib syndrome. Her lungs had filled with fluid and she make no sound that could be heard. The time that followed was so sad for Ruby and Donald. Aubrey, Anna and I flew to California to be with her and it was devastating. Following this her doctor told her she should have another baby soon because that would help her heal, so right away she became pregnant again. After a few months she began to show her pregnancy. After the sixth month passed she could not feel any movement, so she flew to New Orleans to see a specialist. Upon being examined she was told the baby inside was dead. The trauma she suffered was horrible. The doctor also told her that the baby had deteriorated and surgery was not an option, that the infection contained but if surgery was performed the infection would spread to her and she too would die. So she had to carry the dead baby and he would have to induce labor and she would have to give birth normally. Once again I travel to New Orleans to be with her. She went through the delivery and soon as she was able to leave she flew back to California to join her husband.

Between the two of them they decided to try once more to have a child. As time passed she became pregnant and was going to have that much wanted child. This time with no problems she gave birth to a beautiful baby girl. They were so happy with this little girl they decided to try for a son. Only two years passed and sure enough, she was pregnant again. This time as before there was no problem and she gave birth to that son they so desperately wanted. Life was going great for them now. He managed to get stationed in California, and they bought a town house and as the children became old enough they started to school. This really pleased Donald because California was his birth place and quoting him, "California is the best place to live and bring up your children". Ruby agreed with him, but said the only thing wrong with California was it was too far from Mississippi where her family is from. As the children became college age and leaving home Don took his retirement from the Navy with having two children in college and the extra expense. They needed more money than retirement pay so Ruby reminded him that he would need to find a job after that he went to work for a very reliable firm and after a long time retired again. He reminded her that having two retirements that he had retired for good, but another very good opportunity came his way so once again he went back to work. He told her this time I plan to work for the third retirement and besides I have this very rich Aunt and I am one of three beneficiaries but discounting this for now it is no help but we will be fine with three retirements. After a few years and his Aunt had reached her one hundredth birthday. Not long after they celebrated her birthday they received a call saying Aunt Irene had died and after her estate was settled they had become millionaires.

By this time their children were adults, so as he had promised her he would show her the world. He began booking cruises and after the twelfth cruise he had shown her a great part of the world. So in keeping his promise to her on her sixtieth birthday he took her to Paris. She said with all the places he had taken her to Paris was her favorite.

After all the traveling they decided to settle down and build the house of their dreams. As soon as it was finished they moved in. They both expressed that they were still in love and very happy.

They remained in the new house for a few years to her grief Donald getting old began being very sick. As they celebrated their fifty first anniversary he told her he only wished he had fifty one more with her. Shortly after that he died.

Now she is living in that big beautiful house alone. Her children really visit her often and she often ask for grandchildren but to date there are none. They say maybe later. I visit her and she comes to be with me and we talk almost every day.

She related to me recently that after mama died, one night when she went to bed she was so hungry that she got out of bed, went into the kitchen and ate raw oatmeal from the box. I laughed and said, "now you are so rich you could buy the oatmeal factory." We both had a chuckle over that statement. As for me I feel fortunate having lived through it all. I married at a young age and gave birth to my first child at age eighteen. My husband was a good man and was not afraid of hard work. We went through several lean years and did not enjoy many luxuries. We had two other children and we were very proud of our little family, two marvelous sons and a beautiful daughter.

After working on many jobs he decided to join the law enforcement and become a policeman. The pay was nominal so he took on other jobs to make extra money. Things were going fine for a long time and he helped with the children. He was a strict disciplinarian and we reared three good, well behaved children. They were raised with love and the beast of care. But as the years went by he began to be unfaithful to me. As it goes girls seem to like a man in uniform and the temptation began to have an effect on him. For instance the children and I would be in the car and a car would pass in front of us and my son would ask, "who was that in the car with daddy"? Many such instances as that happened and one night a girl called me and wanted to talk. I told her fine and she came to my house. His sister was there and insisted that I not be alone when she came so she kept the children out of the room as we talked. She told me that she had loved him for five years and I let her cry on my shoulder. After that I lost faith in him and when my daughter, the youngest child, became eighteen years old I filed for a divorce and gave him his freedom. He remarried shortly after the divorce. They had two sons afterward giving my children half brothers.

I remained single for nine years owning and operating my own business. Then one day a friend of mine told me she had some one she wanted me to meet. She told me that he was a commander in the Navy and was stationed in the same city that I lived in. I said fine I would like to meet him. So she arranged a blind date for me and then he came to pick me up because we were meeting she and her husband for dinner, I was totally impressed. We became inseperable. We dated for nine years with him saying, "why change good friends into moral enemies", and me answering with, "a burned child is afraid of fire". As time passed I thought that he loved me and I knew I loved him but my pride kept me in tact. One night we had a big disagreement and decided to call it quits so we departed good friends.

Then one night he called me saying he missed me so much he couldn't sleep day or night and could he take me out to dinner and talk. I readily said yes I would, because I was hurting too.

He picked me up and we went to our favorite restaurant. After being seated, he reached across the table, took my hands and said, I love you so much and will you marry me? I was so shocked but readily answered, six months ago I would have said no but tonight I am saying yes.

After dinner he took me home and we were two happy people. We began making plans and were soon married with my oldest son giving me away. We left the wedding party and said we would be going to Pensacola for our honeymoon, but being the devoted mom and wanting my daughter to know where I was I told her that we would be staying in a motel for the night and leave the next morning.

Just as we had gone to bed and things were going great a loud knocking on our door began. He said "What the hell is that", so he quickly got dressed and went to the door. And to our suprise there stood the whole wedding party. They had brought my kids, the deputy sheriff, and all our friends, taunting and shaming us, with my daughter saying shame on you mama, I was an old fashion chivalry and did they ever get a kick out of that. After all the fun and laughter they finally left. Needless to say the mood was over and we went to sleep. The next day we were so happy together and it remained for eleven years, and I expressed to everyone that with this marriage to Rudy was the happiest years of my life. Rudy had been in the Navy for twenty eight years and had gone from joining the Navy when he reached eighteen, going in as a white hat to the rank of Commander. He was recommended for the rank of Captain being a pilot and very brilliant but upon taking a physical examination he was diagnosed as having a heart problem and was losing his promotion to Captain so he decided to retire. After we had been married a few years he had on occasion episodes of angina. One day while at the doctors office he suggested that Rudy have by-pass surgery and that could be corrected so he underwent the surgery. After surgery he did very good and for six years he had no problems. Then one day the chest pain returned and he was advised that he needed heart surgery again so with hesitation he had another operation. This one seemed to work well and he remained optimistic that all was well, and he was fine for a few years. He went about doing what he wanted to do with no problems.

It was near Christmas time and my daughter and I had gone out of town shopping and as we drove back in the driveway we heard this weak voice saying "help". My daughter seeing him first yelled to me, call for an ambulance, Rudy is down. I rushed in and called the emergency number and when we got to the hospital the doctor said "he has had a stroke". He was totally paralyzed on the left side. He told us later that he had gone out for a sandwich and going in the drive-through he dropped his change. He drove back home and almost went through the back of the garage because he could hardly stop the car. He said then he went inside to watch the Notre Dame football game, ate half of the sandwich and realized that he needed to charge the battery in his remote airplane because he and some friends were going to fly their remote airplanes the next day. However while he was in the garage he fell and could not get up. We have a long driveway and he said he yelled for help but no one could hear him. He laid on the concrete floor which was wet because the humidity was so high and his jogging suit was soaking wet. They said his stroke was sever because he did not get to the hospital soon enough. He had laid there for seventeen hours before we came home and found him. He had gone fishing alone the day before and I had no idea that he would have this kind of a problem.

The doctor sent him out of town for therapy. I went often to see him. When allowed I would bring him home but it was so sad when I had to take him back, and I would cry all the way back home having to leave him there. Finally after six weeks they told me they could not help him so he was dismissed and I brought him home. I continued to have a therapist come to our home and work with him but he was never able to gain anything back.

After I brought him home he was given the best care possible. I hired a very gentle man named Felton to care for him while I was at work. He was very sharp mentally and his right side was perfect so I bought him a small cart for the handicapped called a Little Rascal. He could drive it with his right hand so Felton would help him get on it and he could ride all over the neighborhood which he loved.

One day as I was coming home I saw him sitting on his cart with two ladies standing beside him. I stopped and asked if there was a problem. He told me as he was turning around he hit something the driveway of the neighbors house and turned over. He said these ladies helped me get back on my Rascal. I asked are you hurt and he said nothing but my dignity. With that he drove back home as I followed him. Felton was waiting there to help him get off this Rascal.

As he settled in from his ride he told Felton that he needed to get on his potty chair, and in just minutes Felton called me to bring me a cold cloth that Rudy was getting sick, but before I reached him with the cloth Rudy had crumbled to the floor, his hands extended backward and lifeless. I immediately called an ambulance and he was rushed to the hospital. The doctor seeing his position asked me, what do you want me to do, and I said "save his life" so they immediately put him on a respirator. For two weeks I stayed at the hospital only to go home long enough to bathe and change clothes. The doctor finally told me that wen he fell and hit his head he had a blood vessel break in his head causing his brain stem to be broken and after many brain wave test he had no movement and I would have to sign to give them permission to turn the life support machine off. I panicked and said "I can't do that". His two sons were with me and said they would help me, and with that he was gone. The days that followed was the saddest of my life. In my mind I'm wondering how much more can I withstand. Then remembering my faith, if the good Lord take you to it, he will take you through it.

As the friends and families gathered for his funeral it was so sad. As a military man he was given a military funeral. Following the ceremony there was the twenty one gun salute. Then the traditional fly over where one left the formation indicating my precious Rudy had departed. I thought my heart would literally burst sadness. He had asked me at an earlier time when he died he did not want flowers, just his wings for his monument.

So in his honor and fulfill his wish I took his plaque and had his wings removed and cemented at the bottom of his grave. I still go by on occasions and brush away the dust and polish his wings. I still miss him but I know one day I will have my final flight and join him once again.

As I think back over the years I have truly been blessed, to be able to withstand all the heartaches of losing mama, daddy, ten of my brothers, three sisters, and my dear husband Rudy. I know I have been left here for a reason. To have had the good times with each of them and the precious memories.

Now sharing these years of my life gives me a new lease on life and a reason to continue with optimism and a loving attitude that I can share with and depart to others. To live and love and be your very best. Looking back over the years. There was my daddy, a strong and honorable man. He had his hardships to face. And also had his pride and happiness throughout his life. He was my beloved daddy and had my full respect until the end.

Then there was mama. She was my safe place in the midst of the storm. I learned so many things from observing her and by her teaching me about patience and endurance. Not be afraid to meet with challenges as they came my way. To always be stable and to know the meaning of loving and being loved. My brothers were the heroes my life. I always felt secure knowing I had big brothers that would protect me from any harm that might come my way. I grew with the nickname Sugar Baby that was given to me by them which I loved and carried as long as they lived.

My sisters, especially my oldest ones, adored me. They were kind and helpful to me as I grew up. I learned very much from watching them mature into adults. I loved them so and their memory lingers on and on. Now left to embrace the memories of all our beloved family are my little sister Ruby and me. Even though we live a long distance apart we are very close and we communicate often. We love each other dearly. We often discuss our family and are amazed that we are the remaining, and in our hearts and thought, who will be left. Having relived the memories of this our family will remain in our hearts, and the next generation will have a guide to rely on for years.

Printed in the United States
By Bookmasters